IN MY NEIGHBORHOOD

WRITTEN BY
OSCAR LOUBRIEL

ILLUSTRATED BY
ROGÉRIO COELHO

TILBURY HOUSE PUBLISHERS

In my neighborhood, on my side of town,
we don't say it with words, we sing it with sounds.

We don't utter a sentence or mutter a phrase;
We talk to each other in musical waves.

Violin is my brother. He has four soulful strings.
From his curved wooden neck each note bends and springs.

My mother, Piano, has eighty-eight keys.
Her voice stretches, echoes, and floats on the breeze.

My father is Cello, and oh, what a fellow.
The tone of his laugh is low, smooth, and mellow.

But me? My name's Drum. BOOM-CLACK, RAT-A-TAT.
My head is a snare and I wear a hi-hat.

My stomach's a bass drum, my arms are drumsticks, and my only song is CLICK-CLACK, CLACK-CLICK.

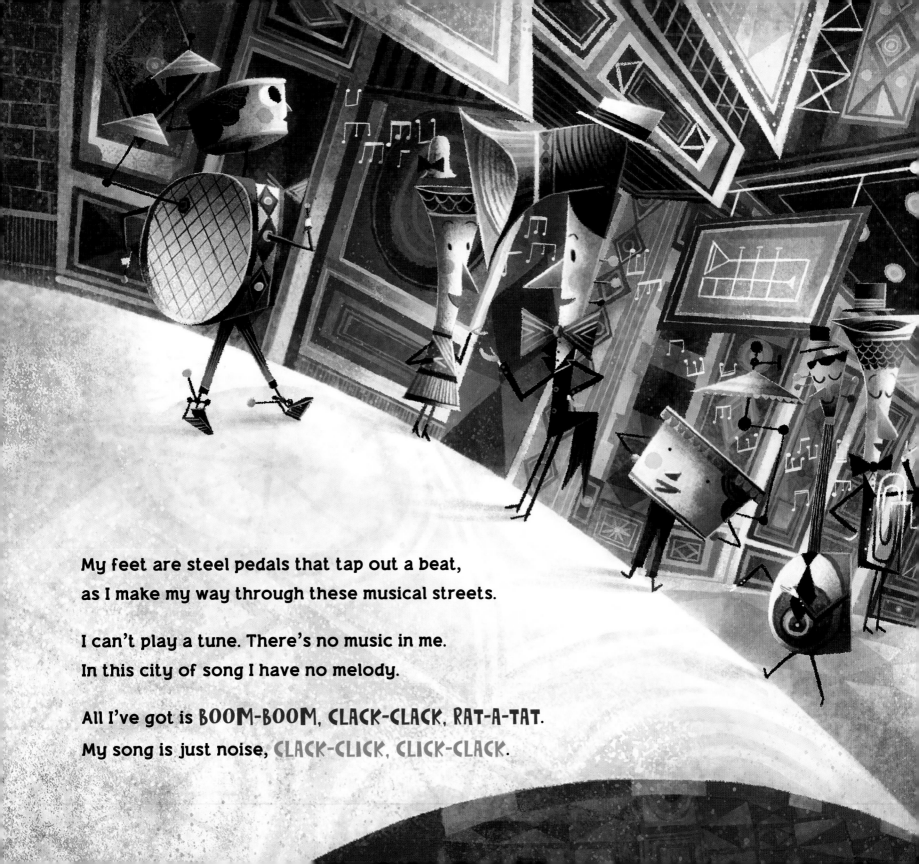

My feet are steel pedals that tap out a beat,
as I make my way through these musical streets.

I can't play a tune. There's no music in me.
In this city of song I have no melody.

All I've got is BOOM-BOOM, CLACK-CLACK, RAT-A-TAT.
My song is just noise, CLACK-CLICK, CLICK-CLACK.

Sounds fill the air of a hot summer day.
Xylophones and marimbas with so much to say

strike bars with their mallets to send out their truths,
stacking phrase upon phrase, some tight and some loose.

Their chatter takes wing on glittering brass,
when tubas and trombones weave their way past.

As I clatter and click toward the city center,
I bump into Baritone, Alto, and Tenor.

These saxophone brothers stop to converse,
asking me, just a drum, if I'd like to rehearse.

They're in need of a rhythm, a tempo, a groove.
My heart skips a beat. I have so much to prove.

So *that's* what a drum does. I now understand.

Can my rhythm and cadence take flight and sail?
Can I lay down a beat for the saxophones' wail?

The moment has come to give it my best,
swing my sticks, rap my steel, put myself to the test.

Yes, I'll drive the train, CLACK-CLICK, CLICK-CLACK,
and I'll keep it on time, BOOM-BOOM, RAT-A-TAT.

I throw down the beat: "1–2–3–**4**!"
My tom drums BOOM and my bass drum roars.

Saxophone notes climb up to the sky,
like fluttering, dancing butterflies.

As we bebop and swing through musical phrases
the crowd on the boulevard listens and gazes.

Hands begin clapping, fingertips snapping.
Bodies are moving, toes begin tapping.

The sky's a bright blue, the sun's shining yellow,
and here comes my father, soulful Cello.

He throws down his bow and slaps his strings,
then my mother adds a pianoing ding.

Now my brother yells, "*I want to join in!*" as a big grin creases his violin skin.

Neighbors on balconies dance, clap, and cheer,
and I'm glad that today I conquered my fear.

I'm roaring my rhythms, singing my song.
If it comes from the heart, the music is STRONG.

In my neighborhood, on my side of town,
we don't say it with words; we sing it with sounds.

Author's Note

I learned to play drums so that I could help make the music at family gatherings, as most of my uncles and cousins are guitarists, pianists, and singers. Music is the world's universal language, and the drummer provides the universal foundation of music. A drum set's percussions channel and shape the conversation among the band's other instruments and vocals, and the band's conversation swells outward to surround and pull in the audience. When it's working, it's the most powerful communication there is.

Like Drum in the story, a drum set reveals its true identity and unlimited potential in use. The bass drum grounds the beat with low notes. The snare drum climbs and soars with high notes. Tom-toms play middle notes with colorful phrasing. The hi-hat controls the timing with strict syncopations, and crash and ride cymbals rise and spread over the rest like a top layer of icing on a cake of sound.

Drumming has taken me all over the world, and I think I have learned this: By doing what you do well, you can shape your own destiny.

Oscar Loubriel is a first-generation Puerto Rican American raised in a musical family in Chicago, surrounded by uncles who were professional guitar players. Given his first drum set at the age of 10, Oscar has been playing ever since in churches, clubs, and concert venues. He toured with high school and college bands, studied music theory, graphic design, and fiction writing, recorded a few albums, and visited fifty countries on five continents while playing drums on cruise ships. This is his third children's book.

Rogério Coelho has illustrated more than 100 books for Brazilian publishers and has twice received the Jabuti Prize, Brazil's top literary prize. His illustrations have been published in England (*Storytime Magazine*) and in the US, where this is his fourth book. His wordless picture book *Boat of Dreams* (Tilbury House, 2017) received starred reviews from *School Library Journal* and *Booklist* and was named a Best Book for Kids 2017 by the New York Public Library.

Text © 2021 by Oscar Loubriel • Illustrations © 2021 by Rogério Coelho

Hardcover ISBN 978-0-88448-701-2

10 9 8 7 6 5 4 3 2 1

Tilbury House Publishers
Thomaston, Maine
www.tilburyhouse.com

Library of Congress Control Number: 2021938216

Designed by Frame25 Productions
Printed in Korea

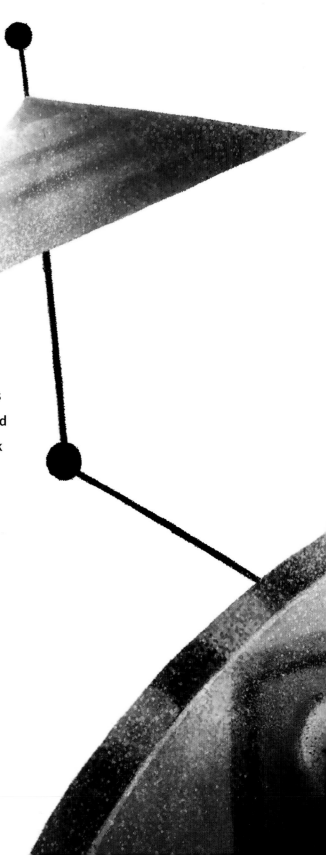

In My Neighborhood
01/15/2022